Prisoner in Alcatraz

by

Theresa Breslin

Published in 2004 in Great Britain by
Barrington Stoke Ltd, Sandeman House, Trunk's Close,
55 High Street, Edinburgh EH1 1SR

Reprinted 2005

ISBN 1-842991-50-7

Printed in Great Britain by Bell & Bain Ltd

A Note from the Author

The island of Alcatraz in the bay of San Francisco was used for many years as a prison for the worst criminals in the United States of America. It was a grim rock fortress with a harsh regime that was both feared and respected.

Not so long ago I visited the now empty prison. I walked along the bleak, echoing corridors. I sat in one of the small cells and stared out through the metal bars. I listened to recordings that prisoners had made, and talked with a former guard who had known the "Bird Man". I heard stories about the prison and the inmates.

The prison on the rock is so famous that several films have been made about Alcatraz. My book is based on real life when a group of prisoners staged a break out in the late 1940s.

If you want more information check out the website: www.nps.gov/alcatraz.

For John H.

Contents

Chapter 1
Alcatraz

Rule Number Five

It is your right to have:

Food, clothing, shelter and medical attention.

Anything else you get is a privilege.

Alcatraz.

The Island.

The Rock.

This is no local state prison. This is a federal prison for crimes against the Nation – the United States of America.

It's stuck right out there near the Golden Gate Bridge. On a big hunk of stone jutting up out of the waters of San Francisco Bay.

Good old San Fran. How does the song go again? You leave your heart in San Francisco. And then it goes on about the little cable cars reaching halfway to the stars.

The one time I came through the city I only caught a glimpse of the cable cars.

I was on my way to Alcatraz. They take the prisoners out there from a pier that's well away from the city. They don't want to disturb the honest townspeople. Don't want to let the folks on holiday see us either. Might spoil the tourist trade. Prisoners ain't a pretty sight. Though, when word gets out there's a new prisoner going over, there's always two or three guys turn up to watch that early morning boat ride.

Why do they come? Does it make them feel better to see us chained up like slave people? Does it make them feel safer as they go back to their nice homes, with the shiny, big car parked out front? Do they feel better because they know another bad man's been locked away? I guess it gives them something to talk about at dinner. Something to say to their neighbours across the fence.

"Hey, guess what, Alvin? I saw a real live murderer today."

Puts a bit of interest into their dull, dull lives.

I remember that boat ride.

All at once the bridge looms up. Not so much Golden Gate as red rust. The big, iron girders arch above us as we go from the city to the national park on the other side. They say the trees there are as tall as the Empire State Building. Then the fog rolls in and I don't see anything any more.

I can hear the seals though. The noise gets louder as we approach the prison jetty on Alcatraz Island. Those big walruses are just sitting on the rocks staring at us and honking.

Saddest sound I ever heard.

I was going to see and hear a lot sadder things in the next months.

But to tell you the honest truth, on that day, I felt sort of proud to be going there.

Crazy, huh?

I mean, I was scared too.

I'd heard all the stories of how tough it was.

And about that Rule Five – the food, water, shelter, medical attention and nothing else thing.

How it was full of guys who'd cut you soon as look at you.

But I was kinda proudful too. I mean, I would be among the big boys now. I hadn't liked it when the judge at my trial had classed me as "a petty thief gone wrong".

"Easily led astray", my lawyer had pleaded in his address to the jury.

It made me look none too bright. As if I didn't have the smarts.

But here I was now.

On that boat.

I was one of the big boys.

The real hoods.

On my way to the most famous prison in the U.S.A.

The most famous prison in the whole wide world.

Alcatraz.

Chapter 2
The Raid

"You don't want to linger too long in them showers, Marty."

I turned quick. Soap still in my eyes.

"What?"

"Pretty young boy like you. Some of these men haven't been near a woman for years, and they're not too choosy, if you get my drift."

I stepped out of that shower stall fast and grabbed my clothes.

It was Taylor. He'd been a prisoner on the Rock since it first opened.

To begin with I liked Taylor. In my first weeks in Alcatraz he helped me, protected me. What I didn't know then was that he'd been told to.

"Look after Marty," they'd said.

What I didn't know was that a certain group of prisoners had been waiting for someone small and skinny like me to show up. They had a plan to escape but it needed someone real thin to squeeze through one of the air vents and along a pipe behind it. I was just the right size.

They waited a month or so and then got Taylor to approach me about their plan.

"Don't want to hear no plan," I said as soon as he began.

I walked away.

I'd had enough of other people's plans. That's how I got in jail in the first place. My friend Jay had a plan. Excuse me. My *ex*-friend Jay had a plan.

I used to live with my ma in a shack near the railway yards. After Ma died they stuck me in a children's home which is where I met Jay. As soon as I could I ran off from that home and went back to the shack. I'd been there about two years on my own when Jay shows up.

He wanted me to help him with a robbery. It was a great plan, so he said.

He had it all worked out. There was this little town miles away. No-one would know us. Only two staff on duty at the bank. The manager and a female clerk.

At lunchtime the manager crossed the street to get his sandwiches and the woman was on her own for about ten minutes. Jay's father and brother were in prison. He needed money to get them a good lawyer. They had told him where he could get some guns.

I wasn't keen.

"I'm not a thief," I said.

Jay laughed. "What do you call it every day when you break into a goods wagon at the railway yards and take stuff? Borrowing?"

"It's just there," I said. "It don't belong to nobody at that point in time. It's just ... passing through."

"Marty King, you live in a world you just made up. It's stealing."

I shook my head. When Ma was alive she never called it stealing. She called it sharing. We never took everything, never cleaned a wagon out. We just took bits and pieces. Enough for us to eat and buy clothes.

"If you plan what to take and sell it for profit, that *is* stealing, Marty," my ma said.

"What we are doing is sharing out. We only take a little from those that can afford it. Just enough to keep us alive."

That's what I told Jay. I said, "I only take from the goods wagons what I need to live. I'm not gonna steal money from a bank. I ain't a thief."

Jay said, "You could do the driving then. You don't have to do the actual stealing. I'll go in the bank myself and get the money. You sit outside in the getaway car."

I shook my head.

"Aw, come on, Marty," said Jay. "You could go down to Mexico and live there and have a farm. You could plant those tomatoes and peppers and all those things you used to tell me about when we were in that children's home together. One little drive, that's all, and you could have all of those things."

I thought about it. When I was a growing boy my ma used to say that one day we'd do that. We'd go down Mexico way. Her and me. At night in the shack she'd sit and talk about how when I was a bit older we'd ride a train proper. Not like the tramps, but with a paid for ticket an' all. Then we'd buy a little place in southern parts where it was warmer, California maybe. We'd get along together just fine, and our plants wouldn't die because there was lots of sunshine and the winters weren't as cold as in Chicago.

Jay had the timings for the raid worked out, but he didn't know anything about road maps and street guides. And he had never learned to write clearly, which meant the map, and the notes, and the name of the bank and the way we were going was all in my writing. Which was bad news for me at the trial later on.

Then Jay gave me a gun. I have to tell you, it felt good when I held the gun. I felt bigger with that gun in my hand. I liked its weight resting right there in my hand and I took to twirling it around like I'd heard the cowboys did in the Old West.

"If you're gonna carry that thing you should know how it works," Jay says as we get to the bank.

While we're waiting outside he shows me the safety catch. Then we see the manager leaving.

"Keep watch," says Jay and goes inside to do the raid.

I stand leaning against the car. It's a cold day. I'm thinking about how good it's gonna be in the south where it's warm. The gun is in my coat pocket. My fingers are playing with the safety catch.

On, off. On, off.

Jay runs out. I should have known something was wrong when I saw him running, but I was watching this little boy with his mom looking in a toy shop window further down the street. And, as I was watching them, I'm still playing with the safety catch.

On, off. On, off. On.

"For Chrissake, Marty! Get in the car!"

I turned. I see a bank guard chasing Jay. Nobody said anything about a bank guard. The guard had a rifle. He fired.

Jay fell down. He was shouting, "I'm dead! I'm dead! He's killed me! I'm dead!"

He wasn't dead. Turned out he'd tripped and broke his ankle. The guard had missed. But I didn't know that then. What with Jay shouting and crying an' all, and the guard raising his rifle again, I panicked. I pointed my gun at him. I didn't mean to shoot anybody or anything, but I pointed my gun and pulled the trigger. The gun leaped in my hand. The guard staggered back. His rifle fell slowly from his hands. I heard it drop. It clattered onto the sidewalk. The bank guard looked down at his chest. I looked at his chest. The front of his jacket was torn apart. A big spurt of red blood came out.

I could hear the child crying and his mom started screaming blue murder. It sounded far away. Like voices on the radio. I didn't speak. Neither did the bank guard. We just stared at each other. I ain't never seen a look like that on a man's face before. He knew he was going to die.

Then everything started to happen very fast. I couldn't keep up with it. The guard fell down. He fell down with an almighty crash. He pitched forwards, *splat*, right at my feet.

A police siren sounded. The woman's screams got louder and louder. Suddenly the noise was all around. As if somebody had flicked a switch and turned the sound on. Her screeching. The police siren coming closer and closer. Wailing and wailing. And the screeching. Right inside my head.

"Shut up!" I yelled. "Shut up! Shut up! Shut up!"

But she wouldn't.

I fired the gun in the air. Just to shut her up.

The bullet bounced off a roof and went through her face.

In 20 seconds I had killed two people.

Chapter 3
Escape Plan

So after all that you see why I wasn't keen on helping out again with someone else's plan.

But Taylor kept on at me.

Gets beside me one day in the prison workshops. Starts whispering in my ear.

"Most of the guys in here would count themselves lucky to be asked to join in a break-out. If you don't take this chance to escape you'll be here for ever. I heard what you done. You done a double murder. That's a death-penalty crime. I'll bet you thought you were lucky you didn't go to the electric chair. Wait till you've been in here a few years. Then you'll wish you'd ended up there. Fried."

"I'm not interested in leaving," I said. "I just got here."

"Yeah. It's OK at the moment. But after a while the boredom will crush you. The never-ending sameness of each and every day. Soon you'll be just like all the others, grabbing a handful of those yellow jacket pills they hand out to help you through the nights."

"I'm not listening, Taylor," I said.

"What you've got to do is simple, Marty. You take a bar of soap. You crawl along the air vent. You stick your hand through the bars at the other end where there's a key hanging. You have to get a print of it in the soap and crawl back. They'll never know it happened."

"Then what?"

"Then someone makes a key from your print in the soap. I got a guy in the workshops can fix that bit of it. Everything else is ready. We jump the guards during the Saturday night film show. We've made these tools – bar separators – to pull apart the bars to the gun gallery. Your key opens the door to the inside cell house.

"We'll grab the guy operating the cell door lever and turn everybody loose. There'll be chaos and panic. Then the four of us will slip away, down to the jetty, grab us a boat and we're off."

"Ain't no-one ever skipped from Alcatraz before."

"That's what they want you to believe," Taylor said. "But a few years back, a con named Dan Hill got away. He worked as a gardener. Just disappeared one day. No-one saw him go."

"I read about that," I said. "He wasn't heard of ever again."

"I think he got away," said Taylor. "He'd told his cellmate that he was making some kind of float out of the bags they delivered the garden manure in."

I shook my head.

"The Warden told the newspapers he must have drowned in the bay. The currents are wicked out there."

"They gotta say something like that," said Taylor. "The police ain't gonna tell us if he did get clear. And he's not gonna phone them up and let them know he's free, is he? I mean, if you made it out, Marty, you ain't gonna wire them saying you're in Oklahoma, are you?"

"No," I said. "I'd go down Mexico way. Send them a card from there."

Taylor gives me an odd look. Then he laughed. "You crack me up, Marty. You really do."

"I ain't getting involved," I said. "The answer is no."

Taylor gave a big sigh.

"The thing is, Marty, you don't have a choice. When Cut Throat Carter asks you to do something, it ain't a question."

"Cut Throat Carter?" I looked at Taylor.

He drew his hand across his neck.

"Carter razors his victims. Slashes their throats. They reckon he'd done about 16 hits for the gangs before the police caught up with him.

"And they say he *likes* cutting up people. Every prison he's been in, there's always some guy gets sliced. You don't want it to be you that gets cut up this time, do you?"

"We only got spoons to eat with," I said. "And the controls here are pretty tight. How'd he get a blade in Alcatraz?"

Taylor puts his finger alongside his nose.

I don't see how even a big time hood like Cut Throat Carter could get his hands on a knife in here.

There are security controls all the time. Random searches. Cell checks. Strip-offs, where they search everywhere, and I mean *everywhere*.

They also use metal detecting machines all over the prison. "Snitch Boxes" they call them. Visitors have to go through one before they're allowed in. Bells start clanging if you're carrying anything metal.

There's a story about the most famous guy that was here – Al Capone. His ma came to see him as soon as he was sent to Alcatraz. There were metal bits in her underwear and they set off the alarms. A wife of one of the prison officers had to body search her.

Old Mrs Capone was so upset she never came back after that. Imagine being in prison all those years and never having a visit from your ma.

****

I was the last out of the workshops that day. We had to walk outside and up some stairs to get back into the main cellblock.

Way over at one end of the prison, behind a high, wire fence, were the houses for the married guards.

On a stretch of grass alongside the washing lines this little kid was throwing a ball.

I watched him for a moment. Remembered playing catch with my ma.

Then the ball bounces up and over his garden fence and rolls right down the outside lane to where the trash is stored. He runs after it.

"Hey, kid!" I yelled. "Throw it this way!"

He looked up.

I smiled and waved.

He waved back.

I beckoned and he came over.

He pushed his little hand through one of the railings on his side, and I reached out.

But the perimeter wire fence on my side was too far away. He had this happy smile on his face. I just wanted to touch him. His skin looked so clean and soft.

Then his mom ran up and grabbed him. I don't blame her. If I had a kid I wouldn't want him looking at the likes of me.

She must have spoken to the guards.

That night they came to my cell and kicked the hell out of me.

"We heard you ain't following the rules, Marty."

"You don't talk, or wave, or even *look* at anybody without permission."

"You don't do anything unless we say so. You understand? Rule Five. All you get is food, clothing, shelter and medical attention."

"Yeah, Marty," one of them added on the way out. "Report to the Doc tomorrow, and make sure you get your medical attention. That's a nasty cut you've got on your head."

"What cut?" I said.

"This one."

And he thumped my face hard against the bars of my cell.

Chapter 4
The Trial

The next day I report to the medical unit.

"What happened to you?" the Doc asked me.

"Walked into a door, didn't I?"

He put stuff on the cut above my eye. Stung like crazy.

Then the Doc stitched my head. Stuck the needle right in. No painkiller first or anything to stop it hurting. I let out a yell.

"You guys," he said. "You blubber over the least thing. Fill other people full of lead but you can't get a simple stitch in your head without making a fuss. I had another con just the same in here last week. Sliced his victims ear to ear, and then screams when I try to lance a boil on his backside."

"You mean Cut Throat Carter?" I said.

The Doc snorted. "Cut Throat Carter indeed. His real name is Brian Winkel."

Save the day! Brian Winkel!

I said to the Doc, "A person would *have* to change their name if it was Brian Winkel. I can see why he done that. You gotta earn yourself some respect."

"Well, there's other ways of earning respect than by changing your name," said the Doc. "You're from Chicago, aren't you? You must have seen the Wrigley Building? It stands up on North Michigan Avenue."

"Sure."

"Mighty grand, isn't it?"

I nodded.

"Wrigley's chewing gum is famous all over the world," the Doc went on, "but with a name like that I'll just bet little boy Wrigley was bullied all through school.

"The way I see it, Mr Wrigley, he could have given up for ever. Being called names all your school life isn't much fun. But no, he upped and founded himself a chewing gum empire. Now he's got the last laugh. I'm guessing, every so often, he flies his very own private jet to the Bahamas. And as he does he'll look down on all those cheap, little houses and think to himself, 'Laugh now, you jerks'."

I said, "I guess he does just that."

The Doc pulls out my file card to write up some medical notes. "Marty King," he reads out my name from the top. “Well, Marty, with a name like that you know you’ve got nothing to prove.”

That’s where he was wrong. I thought I did.

When I was small Ma called me “King of her Heart”. Every Valentine’s day she’d send me a Valentine’s card with those words written on it. “Love to Marty. King of my Heart.”

My pa walked out on us when I was about three. But we got along just fine without him. We stayed in a little shack near the Chicago railway yards and worked the goods wagons.

Those trains were packed full of things to sell in the shops downtown. We moved amongst the trucks and carriages at night, lifting what we could.

Amazing how careless the railway cops were. But then they were used to looking the other way. Most of them were on the take and had deals with the Mob, the big gangs. We stayed well away from that kind of business. Just picked up odds and ends here and there. But sometimes I wondered what it'd be like to get a slice of the real action. To run with the real crooks.

My ma didn't call it stealing, and truth is I never thought of it as such. There wasn't any proper welfare in those days so we would've starved if we hadn't taken stuff. And that isn't right, is it?

The shack was a one room affair but Ma made our little place real homely and pretty. She kept it clean and put up fancy things and pictures cut out from magazines. We grew tomatoes and peppers under the roof window and we got by.

I didn't go to school much. Too tired during the day from working nights. But Ma taught me to read and write. People would come by once in a while to check why I wasn't at school but mainly they didn't bother us. We were white trash and the dogs that roamed around the railway yards scared them.

When I did go to school only one teacher took an interest in me. Her name was Miss Green. She was a thin, strict-looking woman but she never used the cane like the other teachers did. Told us stories instead.

If we worked hard and behaved, come the end of the week we got a story. Old, old stories about ancient Greek and Roman heroes and gods. Every kid in the class loved them. It got so that the tough guys said they'd beat up the rest of us if we got out of line because they didn't want to miss a story. I used to hang around on the outside of the fighting kids. Too small to join in with them, but desperate to be one of the gang.

Miss Green would say to me, "Marty King, you stay away from those bad boys. Don't you be listening to their foolish boasting about how tough they are."

Then Ma upped and died. Her lungs stopped working and nothing could save her. A woman at the hospital where they took her asked me who else was at home.

"Young man," she said, "you need looking after."

She was so nice and helpful I told her the truth, that Pa had run off years ago and there was no-one else. She said she'd fix to take care of me. I really thought she meant it would be her. That she liked me so much she was going to take me to her own home.
Big lies. Big nothing. She fixed me real good.
I got took to a children's home. And you know those things that you hear about children's homes nowadays, well they were all happening in that one, I can tell you.

I had only one friend. That was Jay.
He was older than I was. His ma had died just

like mine, and his father and brother were both doing a long stretch in prison. After a while I thought to myself, *I don't need to be here, I got a home of my own.* So I waited for a chance to skip and I ran away. I knew that the shack would be the first place they'd look, so I went missing for a while. But in the end I made my way back to the railway yards.

The shack had been broken into.
The windows were smashed and the door was hanging by its hinges. The plants had all died and the rain had gotten in and spoiled Ma's pictures. It was overrun with rats, and all my ma's pretty stuff was torn or smashed. I had to stay on there though. I had nowhere else to go.

It wasn't so good doing the trucks at night without Ma and I got real lonesome. So when Jay showed up I was ripe and ready to listen to him. Him, with all his wild tales of how it was going to be so good, and how rich we'd both be.

He turned out to be a liar. He lied about the raid being easy. He lied at the trial. He said it was all my idea. The weasel. He told the cops that I'd done the planning. Showed them my writing on the map and everything. Made it look bad for me.

I should have gone to the electric chair but something came up. Would you believe it?

The teacher Miss Green read about me in the newspaper. Came forward as a character witness, to tell them all I was really a good guy. Stood right up in that witness box and said what a trusting boy I was. She said I was easily led. She said I lived in a fantasy land where I believed in goodness. And it was the world that had let me down, not the other way around.

I liked that. Didn't like so much the bit where she said I couldn't possibly have planned the raid. It sounded as though I was slow-witted.

"Impossible for him to have done this," she told the judge. "This boy doesn't have the brains to think up such a plan."

She went on quite a long time and I didn't understand half of what she said.

"Marty, do you agree with what Miss Green, your character witness, is saying about you?" the judge asked me.

I looked from Miss Green to him, and back to Miss Green again.

"What?" I said.

"See what I mean?" said Miss Green. "He's not with us. He hasn't the wits to plan a raid like this."

My lawyer put me in the witness stand. "Look like you're sorry for what you've done," he said. "Don't say much. Cry if you can."

Well, that was easy. I remembered the woman standing outside the bank with her little boy, and how my bullet had gone into her face. That made me real sad.

The woman was killed by my bullet that bounced off the roof. "A ricochet", they called it. I didn't even know what a *ricochet* was. I had to ask someone later. But I did cry. I thought of that little child without a mom. I knew how he felt. My lawyer, he told me to speak out. So I did. I told them all about my ma and the shack and how we had nearly starved in the winters.

My lawyer kept cutting in on me. He kept changing what I was saying. Putting it into fancy words.

"Look at this half-starved boy," he thundered. "For a true-born American lad to live like that is a shame on our society!"

Boy he was good! I almost believed him myself. He said my pa had been killed in the

War, which was a big lie. But it made everybody listen. "One of our fallen heroes", he called him.

Well, the fallen bit was true for sure. Before he went off, Pa was falling over almost every night of the week. Dead drunk.

So I didn't go to the electric chair. I got two life sentences instead. But the story wasn't over. Oh no.

I'm on my way to the state prison with this other guy and the thing is, my guard who's a kind man, and said I reminded him of his own son, hasn't put handcuffs on me on account of my wrists being so skinny and all. He's got his gun so he reckons everything is fine.

We're walking out to the van and the second guard turns back for some reason, so this other prisoner that's with us wallops my guard on the side of the face with his two fists and then kicks his head when he's down and yells to me, "Look we ain't gonna get a chance like this again. You and me, Marty, we're in this together. Let's go!"

So I went. We jumped in the van and I drove it as fast and as far as I could. That was a mistake. I drove it into the next state. Right into a telegraph pole. Stealing a car and taking it into another state is not just a local crime. It's a crime against the United States. Big stuff. You get sent to a United States prison, not the local state one.

I said it was an accident.

They said I was "hard set on a life of crime, incorrigible".

Incorrigible. I had to ask about that word too.

Meant they put me down for Alcatraz. While I was waiting to go there, the other cons in with me told me they were jealous. Only the big-shots went to the Rock they said.

It was where they'd sent Floyd Hamilton, the guy who drove for Bonnie and Clyde, and Al Capone, and the Bird Man, and Machine Gun Kelly, and all the rest.

"You'll be with the big-time boys, Marty," they said. "Wish it was us."

And I believed them.

Chapter 5
Cut Throat Carter

"That's a nasty wound you got there, Marty."

Taylor's standing beside me in the exercise yard.

I touch my forehead where the Doc gave me my stitches but I don't say a thing.

"Cut Throat Carter heard what happened," he says, "and he's upset for you. Thinks it's unfair. You being new and not knowing the rules." He pats my shoulder. "He says to tell you not to worry, Marty. He'll take care of the guard who split your face."

Which I don't see how he can, seeing as how Carter is a prisoner like the rest of us.

A few days later that guard has to be taken on the boat over to the hospital in San Francisco.

He's got gut rot.

He's sick for a month or more.

I know the guards eat food that's been prepared in the kitchens by the prisoners. I also know these prisoners are the most trusted and are watched non-stop.

But there you are, that's what happened.

I began to think, *This Carter knows all the right people.*

Next thing that happens is Carter himself comes up to speak to me.

As soon as he's near, the guys I'm standing with melt away.

All at once I'm on my own with a lot of space around me in the exercise yard and I have to say I'm a bit nervous.

He nods.

I nod back.

"Thanks for sorting out that guard."

My voice comes out a lot more squeaky than I intended.

"That's OK, Marty," he says, very softly. "That's something I'm good at," he pauses, "sorting people that need sorted."

He doesn't say anything after that but he doesn't move away either.

He's making me feel real fearful.

I think I'd better say something, so I open my mouth.

But before I can speak, Carter says, "Taylor was saying you didn't believe I could slash anyone in this here prison."

Now I'm really scared.

I stammer, "Not exactly, Mr Carter. I just said that it might be hard to get hold of a knife, what with the guards watching us so close all the time."

"So you think I wouldn't be able to stick someone exactly where I want them?"

He leans right close to me.

"Say just about there?" And he stretches out one finger and places it so lightly on the side of my neck.

I gulp. My eyes are staring. I don't move. I don't breathe.

Then he laughs and takes his hand away.

"You're right, Marty," he says. "How could I possibly arrange anything like that?"

I relax a bit.

He steps back and leans against the wall.

He looks at me to be sure I'm watching him, then he turns and signals to Taylor who's standing a little way off.

Right away every guy in the yard is shouting and yelling and screaming and they bunch up into a crowd in the centre of the yard.

The guards on the wall start blowing whistles and the bells go off. The guard in the watchtower fires a shot above our heads.

At once all the prisoners go quiet. They break up into little groups of one or two and drift away to stand beside the walls.

Except for one man.

He's lying on the ground.

Right in the middle of the yard.

There's a knife sticking out of the side of his neck.

Chapter 6
Lock Down

So I'm in this escape plan. Whether I like it or not.

That night I lie on my bed and listen to the pipe banging and the whispering – the prisoners sending messages to each other between the cells.

I'm thinking, *Ain't it so true what Miss Green once said to me*, "Once you've done one bad thing, another follows right after. It's a slippery slope on the road to crime."

I've got no choice now. If I was in any doubt the guys in the cells all around are calling to me.

"It was a set up, Marty. To warn you to do what Cut Throat Carter says."

I'd worked that one out myself. I'm not stupid.

"That guy. The one that got stuck? He's gonna make it. Next one won't be so lucky."

"You don't need a knife to cut a guy," someone else tells me. "They used a sharpened spoon."

Nobody fingered anybody for the stabbing. Nobody spoke up, not even the guy that got stuck. We don't betray each other, us cons. That's what they say. As if it were some kind of noble thing. But of course, the truth is no-one tells because everyone knows that the first man to speak up would be the next one to get knifed.

All the prisoners were locked in their cells for a week as punishment. No work. No play. No showers. No exercise. Food was sandwiches eaten in our cells. Which didn't bother me too much, though some others made plenty of fuss. That was the one good thing about prison as far as I was concerned. Maybe the only good thing. I got fed regular. Which was new for me.

But we get our own back on them guards for all the hard time they gave us. We keep up the whispering through the nights. Calling wolf whistles. Yip, yip, yipping, and baying. The sound echoes around those cellblocks, sadder than the foghorn we hear outside. Makes the hairs on the back of my neck stand up, I can tell you.

And the whispering, always the whispering.

"Look out, Mr Guard."

"We're coming for you."

"One day we'll catch you by surprise."

"There's someone behind you."

"Don't turn around ... around ... around ..."

Chapter 7
Dining Hall Riot

The air vent they want me to go through is on the wall of the dining hall. It goes a little way back and then turns a sharp right and runs along the wall to the end where it feeds into the main shaft.

Opposite this junction is the wall of the cell house control room where the key hangs.

At break times Carter and Taylor and Frank "Slugger" Malone, the other con who's breaking out with us, tell me what I've got to do.

“Once we heave you into that vent, you turn right, Marty. Got that? Crawl to the back and then go right.” Carter holds up his right hand.

“Right,” I say. And I point in the same direction.

But he’s facing me so that means I’m actually holding up my left hand.

“Hey, this is my left hand, isn’t it? Say that again.”

Frank grinds his teeth. Carter moves to stand beside me so that we are facing the same way. He explains it once more slowly. They go over and over it a million times.

Gets so my head is sore and I tell them, “No more. Don’t tell me any more.”

“We’ve spent years planning this,” snarls Frank. “I don’t want it messed up by a dumb kid.”

He lunges at me. He's got hands like shovels. He grabs my jacket and lifts me right up off the ground.

Taylor steps between us.

Carter looks towards the guards patrolling on the wall above.

"Take it easy," he says quietly. "The kid's going to do all right." He reaches out and strokes my cheek. "Sure you are, Marty."

Somehow I'm more scared of him patting my face than Frank grabbing my jacket with his big paws.

They arrange for a riot in the dinner hall.

Everybody's in on it. Even the ones who don't want to make a run for freedom. We're all just happy to be causing trouble.

Anything to liven up the boredom of days that are always and for ever the same.

The same food at the same time every day, the same conversations again and again.

I've only been in the place for a few months, and already I am fed up and sick to the back teeth of hearing the same old jaw on and on and on.

In the middle of supper one night, someone at the top end lifts their plate and chucks it at the wall shouting, "I ain't eating this pigs' swill!"

Two seconds later 50 more men have done the same. The benches are up and they're yelling and hammering, clattering their spoons on mugs and plates.

"Get to the doors!" yells the senior officer to his team. "Lock them in!"

They're out in seconds and the door slams shut behind them.

As soon as they're out of the room, Frank starts unscrewing the cover of the air vent.

Taylor grabs my clothes and fast as you like I'm buck naked in the pipe, crawling like crazy. And yes, I'm skinny, but this is a tight squeeze, I'm telling you.

"You've only got about eight or nine minutes!"

That's what Taylor and Frank had said.

That's how long it takes the guards to let off the tear gas to break up a riot.

I crawl along to the junction and I look up.

I see a beautiful sky above me. Blue sky I see, and I think, *What's to stop me climbing up there? Nothing. I'm the only one small enough to escape this way. I could breeze right on out of here by myself. Maybe.*

I wait just about ten seconds, feeling so good that I can breathe fresh air again. And there's no-one watching me breathe.

Then I remember that guy on the ground in the exercise yard with the knife in his neck. I edge across the gap and peer through the bars into the control room.

Carter had it worked out just right. The officer there has gone to help the others. The vent here hasn't got the meshed cover like those on the prisoners' side. The bars are far enough apart for me to stick my hand through.

I reach for the key.

Footsteps running.

I stop.

The door opens.

I can't get my hand back in time.

A guard runs in.

I'm lying with my face pressed against the vent, hand stuck right out there in the air.

The guard picks up a cosh lying on the table, runs back out.

I start breathing again.

I press the key into the soap. Both sides. Carefully. Stretch my hand back out and return the key.

I'm along that passage faster than I came.

What a welcome I get! Almost worth doing it for that alone.

Carter says to leave the soap bar in the air vent to collect later. Frank screws the cover back on and gives the screwdriver to a con who's agreed to take the rap for having it on him. I get into my prison uniform and the prisoners tell the guards they'll surrender before the tear gas is let off.

The guards are full of it. How we gave in. How they stopped a riot in under 15 minutes.

I'm almost singing. All the men want to know me. Shake my hand. Me. Marty King.

Carter slaps me on the back. “You’re a smart boy, Marty, and no mistake.”

For the first time in my life I’m a big hero.

Chapter 8
In Solitary

There was some real hard time done in Alcatraz after the dining hall riot.

All privileges were taken away.

The guards checked us night and day. Cells searched. Mattresses ripped open, pillows taken apart. Body searches. Full cavity examinations and none too gentle with it either. Looking to see if you'd hidden anything where the sun don't shine.

The stuff them guards come up with during the searches, you wouldn't believe.

You've no idea what a man can hide, and the places he can hide it.

One prisoner had tiny strands of wires tucked up right under his eyelids. Another had little pieces of metal tucked in-between his teeth. They said Houdini used to do that. That's how he could pick locks when he was tied up and spring the padlocks on his chains.

Taylor and Cut Throat Carter sure were smart to think to leave the soap with the key impression on it sealed up in the ventilation duct.

Every man who'd been in the dining hall that day got a spell in solitary. They call it "the hole". The long-timers hate it and say you can go mental in there.

The solitary cells are on D block and ain't got no bars, just a 200 pound solid steel door. Food is pushed through via a swivel unit at floor level. There's a window for the guards to look in on you, but it's got a panel that clips over so they can keep you in complete darkness.

I done my time in solitary. It sure does mess with your head. No daylight. No night-time. No time of day. Nothing.

My ma comes to visit me one night.
I don't know how she gets in. Don't recall the cell door opening, but all at once there she is, sitting on the floor beside me. She smiles but she doesn't speak. She looks young and pretty. When you're a youngster yourself and growing, you don't ever see your ma as a female-type woman. You don't notice whether she's good-looking or how old she is. It's as if she has no age at all. She's just your ma, and she's always there. Until one day she's not.

When she came in my cell I wasn't sure if she'd like me to talk to her. I mean I knew she wasn't real, not properly anyway. But I thought maybe she was lonesome on the other side, and her spirit had called by for some company and conversation. So I began to catch her up with my news, about Jay and how things had gone a bit wrong for me.

The guard passing my food through the hatch must have heard me, and he says, "Who are you talking to in there, Marty?"

My ma puts a finger to her lips. I see that she doesn't want the guards to know she's there. So I just laugh and say, "Why, no-one. No-one at all."

But I know that I'll have to whisper now when I'm talking to her so the guards don't hear me.

The next day I get a visit from the Doc. He examines me all over and talks to me a bit. Then he asks me who I've been speaking to lately. I just wink and tap my nose.
He turns to the guard.

"I want this boy out of here."

The guard replies, “That’s the Warden’s decision.”

The Doc glares like he’s in a bad mood. But I tell the Doc I’m doing OK. He says to me softly, “Have you got someone with you in here, Marty?”

I look over his shoulder at Ma and she nods, so I know it’s all right to tell him about her being there.

The Doc listens to me for a while then he gives me a shot in the arm.

When I wake up I’m in the medical unit. I’m not too good for a few days. It’s as if my brain went on vacation and left me behind. I forgot who I was even. I stare at the ceiling and the light comes and goes. I hear the boats passing and the foghorn sounding and that fine, white sea mist seeps in right up to my neck, blanking me out.

The Doc makes me get up every day, and gives me easy chores to do about his clinic, and slowly the fog moves away.

In the end, things quieten down in the prison. The guards let the heat off a bit.

One day word comes from Taylor. The key is made.

We're set to break out!

Chapter 9
Break for Freedom

Carter won't give the go-ahead.

He wants to do the jump in the middle of the movie show. But since the riot the guards have been doubling up on shifts and being more careful. And we haven't had a movie since way back, so we've got to wait.

Frank is mad crazy to get on with it. Every exercise break he keeps nagging away at Carter, until one day Carter takes him aside in the yard and speaks to him serious like. I watch them. I see how Carter folds

Frank's collar back carefully as he is talking. As if his only concern is that Frank looks tidy. Then I see his hand slip under Frank's chin. I see his fingers draw a line along Frank's throat.

They move apart and Frank walks towards me. He's got a mean look on his face. He kicks at my legs as he goes by. But I can see he's as scared of Carter as I am.

Christmas comes and goes. Then New Year. New Year's Eve I hear fireworks and music and people laughing and dancing from way across the water. I never thought the sound of folks having a good time would be a lonesome sound. But I tell you it was.

Then one day Carter says, "Tonight's the night." And truth is, it's a bit of a shock to me.

I think, *Maybe I don't want to go.* I work in the laundry now. Washing and ironing uniforms is big business for the prison so you can make some nickels and dimes if you get picked for that job. Alcatraz does all the laundry for the military on the West Coast and I got me a good position there. Besides which I'm eating three meals a day. My belly's fuller than ever it was in the whole of my life before. Plus we're back to having a movie once a month. Guys gripe because they don't ever show movies with criminal activity or sex in it. But I never complain.

I don't admit this to no-one, but up until I went to prison, I ain't never seen no movie before. I like the movies a lot.

"Could you wait right to the end until the movie's over?" I said. "I been looking forward to that Shirley Temple one for a long time."

I think Frank is gonna smack me in the face.

But Taylor laughs.

"You're kidding. Ain't you, Marty?" He turns to Carter. "He's full of stupid wisecracks."

Carter gives me a hard look. "Yeah, right," he says.

Saturday night, in the middle of the movie, they jump the two guards.

It kind of slipped my mind that this was the night. I'm looking at the picture on the screen. Shirley Temple's up there singing, with little fancy bows in her hair and those sweet dimples. Carter gives the signal and everybody is on their feet. Except me, that is. I hang back, looking up at Shirley. Carter grabs my sleeve. I drag my eyes away.

Fast as a whip, Frank cracks one guard's skull against the wall. The guard's head snaps back. His eyes are still open but you can tell he can't see anything. They pull the gun from the other one, a younger man called John Jefferson Adams.

There were fewer than 20 men at the show that night. Carter tells them if they want to get out they must do exactly as he says. I notice when he talks, they listen. He gives the tools to pull the bars apart to one guy, tells him to use them to break into the gun gallery and then give out the guns. He sends six others to the control room, where there's one big lever that unlocks all the cells. They must overpower the guard there and turn everybody else loose.

Then Carter nods at Frank and Taylor and me. He pushes John Adams ahead of him and the four of us run down towards the laundry.

The guard tries to reason with us.

"Look, guys," he says. "The next gate is locked, and the guards on this side don't carry the key. So I can't open it for you. You can't get through here."

"That's where you're wrong, Mr Adams," sneers Carter. "We got the key."

The guard does a double take when he sees the key in Carter's hand, but he's still confident.

"That only lets you out of the cellblock into the laundry rooms. You can't get to the outside entrance from there."

"We ain't going that way."

Taylor and I look at each other. First we heard of this.

"What way are we going, Carter?" I say.

Carter takes no notice.

He turns back to the guard.

"How many men on the roof?" he asks.

John Jefferson Adams shakes his head. "I ain't telling you," he says.

Carter goes over to him and puts the knife against his chest.

"Do you want to die?" he asks him.

Adams shakes his head. “No, sir, I don’t,” he says.

“Tell me then, how many men on the roof?”

“Two or three,” Adams says quickly. “But if they think the break-out is contained inside the cellblocks, they might bring guards down from the roof.”

“Thank you.” Carter’s voice is very soft. “If you’re a praying man,” he says, “you’d better pray.” He brings his knife up under the guard’s throat.

The guard loses his cool. It’s an awful thing to see and hear.

“Please, sir. Please don’t use that knife on me. I got family. I got kids.”

Carter smiles. “You hear that, boys? You hear how respectful this guard is now? He’s calling me ‘sir’. And do you know why that is? Why, it’s because I have this here knife in my hand and he's scared I might do something like this."

And, so casual, as if he's popping the cork off a soda bottle, Carter leans over and he cuts the guard's throat.

Me, I think I'm gonna faint. I have to sit down, quick, on the ground.

Taylor's face turns three colours of green. "You shouldn't have done that," he says.

"Well, I just did," said Carter.

"Come on!" yells Frank. "We gotta move."

"Yeah," said Taylor. "Let's go."

Carter smiles again. He points to me and Taylor and says in a voice like steel, "You two ain't going anywhere."

Chapter 10
Shoot Out

Carter steps over to one of the big wash boilers.

"Frank and I are going up and out beside the big water pipes right here. A few years ago, when they got more laundry work, they built a whole new set of pipes coming down from the water tower. I happen to know where they feed into the boilers."

"And me," Taylor stammers. "What about me?"

"The boat we got waiting off the jetty is just for Frank and me," Carter says to Taylor. "You're too old. You couldn't swim that far."

Taylor's jaw goes slack. Like he's been punched in the belly. "I helped you," says Taylor. "I helped get the key made."

"Thanks for that," said Carter. "I appreciate it."

He smiles that soft smile of his and says, "And you and Marty No Brains here are going to do Frank and me another favour. You're going to hold the guards up when they break through to this place. That will give us a bit of time to get clear. He came over and bent down to where I was sitting on the floor. He pulled my head back. "Ain't ya?"

I nodded. I couldn't open my mouth. Thought I'd be sick.

Him and Frank bust open a metal panel behind one of the boilers, climb inside and disappear up to the water tower on the roof.

"Marty, we're in trouble," says Taylor, after they've gone. "Big trouble."

It don't take a genius to work that out.

"Only one thing we can do," said Taylor, "that might count in our favour."

I'm not too clear what that means but he seems to expect me to agree, so I nod.

"We need to make it look as if they beat us up," says Taylor. "Then we can say they *made* us help them."

"OK," I said.

"You'll remember to say that afterwards?" Taylor asks me. "When they ask you, you must tell them that Carter and Frank forced us to go this far with them."

It sure annoys me the way people tell me a thing six or seven times. "I get it," I say. "I get it."

Taylor goes over and takes the cosh from the belt of that poor, dead guard.

"So that it looks right, we gotta cosh each other with this and knock each other right out. You do me first, then I'll do you." He hands the cosh to me and turns round so that I can swipe the back of his neck. "Hit me real hard, Marty. Make it look good."

It's only when Taylor is lying out cold at my feet that I see the flaw. Who's going to cosh me? It takes me a while to work out what I have to do. The guards have almost cut through from the main hall before I have a plan.

I have to take at least three runs head-on, hard against the wall, before I do myself enough damage to make it look like Carter and Frank beat me up bad.

Meanwhile Carter and Frank have made it to the roof.

But that's all the distance they got.

Turns out that John Jefferson Adams was braver than we thought. He'd lied to Carter when he said that there were only two guards on the roof and that they'd bring them down if there was trouble inside the jail. There were at least four on roof patrol, and John Adams knew that when the alarm went off, the first thing the Warden would do was send more men up there. So when Carter and Frank popped their heads out of that there water pipe, the guards took them like two rabbits coming out of a burrow.

Police boats in the bay arrested their friends who were waiting to pick them up. Carter had planned to escape from the side of the island that faced the open sea. At that time of day the current would be flowing out to sea and they hoped they'd be carried along with it. They weren't heading for the jetty at all. They guessed that none of the other prisoners would get out of the prison, but if they did they'd run to the jetty on the San Francisco side of the island.

Carter and Frank never intended to take Taylor and me with them. They only needed us to get the key and get it made.

So much for us cons sticking together.

Chapter 11
Locked in for Life

It was all in the newspapers.

Months later we got to see the pictures and read the reports. The newspapers showed the dead bodies of Frank and Carter up close. They looked to me as if they might have been shot in the back. But I don't say nothing.

I reckon I got a break. The guard who Frank slugged down during the movie show recovered. He said his memory was that I didn't want to take part. I had to be pulled along by Carter. So he believed the story Taylor and I gave out that it was nothing to do with us. I lost a couple of teeth when I smashed my face against the wall. So that made it all the more convincing I guess. There was no-one to contradict the story anyway. All the other witnesses being dead.

Every night now I shuffle over and stand like all the others holding out my hand when they come round with the yellow jackets, them sleep pills they give you. I don't sleep so good, see. I dream about the young guard, John Jefferson Adams, pleading with Carter for mercy, begging for his life. I remember the kid I saw playing with the ball at the prison officers' quarters. Was that his kid?

I could've had children. They might have been real cute. Like the little boy who was looking in the toyshop window that day outside the bank. The day I killed his mom.

Folk in here still talk dumb.

"Next break-out, we'll make it."

"I'll get that Warden one day, you'll see."

"I got friends on the outside. Links to the big gangs. They're gonna bust me out of here soon."

New prisoners arrive. You can see that they think they've reached the top. Just like I did. Coming to the most famous prison in the world. Joining the worst criminals in the U.S. of A.

Alcatraz.

Big Deal?

Big Dump.

Big names?

Bunch of losers.

Al Capone. Old Scarface. He eventually died of venereal disease. Before my time, but Taylor told me about him. By the time they shipped him out, Capone's body was wasted away. All maggoty inside. Mind crumbled like mouldy cheese. Bit of him rotted to a stump. Believe me you don't want to know.

And as for the celebrated Bird Man of Alcatraz – he wasn't really. That name was a fraud. Not many people know this. Never had no birds in Alcatraz. He came from Leavenworth Prison to Alcatraz. He kept his birds at Leavenworth. Don't sound as good though, does it? Bird Man of Leavenworth. Ain't got the same ring as Bird Man of Alcatraz.

He went nuts in the end. I looked after him for a while when I worked in the medical unit. I wonder what he might have been out in the world. Learning all those different languages like he did. Knowing all that stuff about birds and all. He could have been famous. People would have travelled miles to see him. Would have paid lots of money to get him to cure their pet parrot or whatever, if it was sick.

Those gangsters have all passed on, like the waters in San Francisco Bay. Cut Throat Carter, Slugger Malone, all those famous names. But that's the long and the short of it. It was their *names* that were famous, not them.

They were just deadbeats really.

They've all gone.

All except me.

Years and years and years I've seen come and go, and I'm still here. I got my plants, tomatoes and peppers and other things I'm allowed to grow. I guess you could say I made it to the Californian sun, but I sure wouldn't want my ma to see her boy now. I wouldn't be King of her Heart no more.

I'm King of the Rock.

Here I am.

And here I'll be until the day I die.

Prisoner in Alcatraz.

Barrington Stoke would like to thank all its readers for commenting on the manuscript before publication and in particular:

Julie Carss
Chris Cooper
Mark Dunphy
Victoria Hill
Alison McDowell
Deirdre Michelucci
Luke Philcox
Ellen Prangnell
Kayleigh Thain
Luke Thomas

Become a Consultant!

Would you like to give us feedback on our titles before they are published? Contact us at the address below – we'd love to hear from you!

Barrington Stoke, Sandeman House, Trunk's Close,
55 High Street, Edinburgh EH1 1SR
Tel: 0131 557 2020 Fax: 0131 557 6060
E-mail: info@barringtonstoke.co.uk
Website: www.barringtonstoke.co.uk

If you loved this book, why don't you read ...

Before Night Falls

by Keith Gray

ISBN 1-842991-24-8

"Let's just say she has been bitten by a vampire ... It means she's one too, doesn't it? And she'll wake up when it gets dark. And she'll come after us."

Andy's camping trip is fast turning into a nightmare. They're soaked and lost ... and when his girlfriend, Lucy, wanders off on her own, things go from bad to worse. She's found alive, but with strange marks on her neck. Could she have been bitten by a vampire?